The Christmas Wish

As soon as she walked in, Erin could tell there was something wrong. "What's happened?"

"Mr Benn didn't make a will," Mum told her and Charlie. "And his nephew says he doesn't know anything about Mr Benn intending to leave the donkeys' fields to us."

"But that's awful," said Charlie.

"We've got twenty-five donkeys to look after," cried Erin. "What are we going to do?"

No one had any answers.

Look out for more books by Sylvia Green!

Sylvia Green

The Christmas Wish

Illustrated by Sophie Keen

SCHOLASTIC

For all the donkeys at the
Isle of Wight Donkey Sanctuary

Scholastic Children's Books,
Commonwealth House, 1–19 New Oxford Street,
London, WC1A 1NU, UK
a division of Scholastic Ltd
London ~ New York ~ Toronto ~ Sydney ~ Auckland
Mexico City ~ New Delhi ~ Hong Kong

First published by Scholastic Ltd, 2004

ISBN 0 439 95890 3

Printed and bound by AIT Nørhaven A/S, Denmark

2 4 6 8 10 9 7 5 3 1

Chapter 1

Benedict

"Charlie! Why are you wearing a pink flowery hat?" Erin nearly dropped the carrot she was holding when she spotted her friend coming across the field.

Charlie grinned as he peered at her from under the huge brim. "I thought I'd try and cheer Benedict up."

"What?"

"We thought he might be missing his previous owner, didn't we?" said Charlie. "And I remembered that she was always wearing hats. So here I am. What d'you think, Benedict?"

The little donkey ignored him and took the piece of carrot from Erin. He chewed on it slowly without any real enthusiasm.

Erin laughed. "He doesn't seem very impressed."

"Come on, Benedict," said Charlie, stroking his neck. "Why won't you try and make friends?"

"Mum's really worried about him not settling in," said Erin.

Benedict had arrived at the Westfield Donkey Sanctuary, which was run by Erin's parents, several weeks ago. He was a lovely grey donkey, beautifully marked with a brown stripe along his back and another across his shoulders making the distinctive "donkey cross".

But ever since he'd arrived he'd just stood on his own every day, ears back, looking dejected. He refused to mix with any of the other donkeys and completely ignored all of the humans. Erin had spent as much time with him as she could, hoping he would bond with her, but so far she'd had no success.

"It's strange," said Erin, stroking Benedict's soft nose. "Donkeys are usually very sociable animals."

"Well, at least, the vet said there's nothing wrong with him," said Charlie.

Erin nodded. At first they'd just thought he was miserable being kept on his own in the isolation unit. New intakes were always put in there for the first few weeks while they were checked over. But he'd been with the rest of the donkeys now for three weeks and he was no different.

"His previous owner did tell us that he's been moved around several different homes in the past," said Erin. "Mum thinks that could be the reason he's not settling here."

"You mean, he's expecting to be moved on again any minute?" said Charlie.

"Yes, so he probably thinks it's not worth making friends," said Erin. "He'll only miss them when he moves – like perhaps he's missing some old friends now."

"Poor little donkey," said Charlie. He patted Benedict's shoulder. "But you're all right now you're here, Benedict. We're going to find a way to make you happy again."

Erin and Charlie left him and walked across the field. Arthur, a dark brown donkey, came trotting over to them. He was closely followed, as usual, by Clover. The two children made a fuss of both of them.

"Hey, Arthur!" Erin exclaimed, jumping back. One of Arthur's favourite tricks was trying to bite the toggles that fastened her coat. "We don't want you swallowing one of those."

Arthur had been the first donkey they'd taken in, when his elderly owner had died. Next had come Clover, a pretty white donkey with light brown spots. Her owners had moved and no longer had anywhere to keep her. From the first day she'd been put in the field she had followed Arthur everywhere.

John, Paul, George and Ringo were four ex-beach donkeys. They were having a pow-wow in the middle of the field. The other donkeys were in various small groups, apart from Tapestry who was enjoying a good roll.

"Oh, I meant to tell you," said Charlie. "When I came past the senior barn, Peanut was trying to pull Whisky's rug off."

"Not again," said Erin. "We'd better sort them out."

They made their way over to the senior barn where the five older donkeys lived. They had their own smaller field, which allowed them access to their barn. Each of them had their own special rug in the winter to keep them warm.

Peanut looked up as they went in. "Sorry, mate," Charlie said to him. "But I've told on you."

Peanut hadn't managed to pull the rug right off and Erin soon fixed it back in place. "There you are, Whisky. All snug again."

Charlie rubbed Peanut's shaggy brown head. "You're an old terror! No one would think you're over forty."

Whisky gave Peanut a gentle nudge with her nose. Erin chuckled. It was lovely to see them being playful. Her parents had rescued Peanut and Whisky from a market. They'd been in a terrible state of neglect and it had taken some time to get them back into good condition and to win their trust.

"Your mum and dad did a great job with these two," said Charlie. "Where are they, by the way?"

"They've gone to meet Mr Benn's nephew," Erin told him. "He's moved into Mr Benn's house and he's asked them to go over there."

Mr Benn had lived in the old farmhouse that was across the other side of the fields. The fields belonged to him and he'd rented them out to Erin's parents for the donkey sanctuary. Unfortunately he had died suddenly three weeks ago.

"Mr Benn promised to leave the fields to the donkey sanctuary in his will," said Erin. "So I suppose Mum and Dad have got to sign some legal papers or something."

"That was good of him," said Charlie. "But then Mr Benn really loved the donkeys, didn't he?"

Erin nodded. "He was always over here."

They walked back towards the house. There were twenty-five donkeys in the sanctuary now and Erin's mother let two rooms out for bed and breakfast to help fund it. Her dad was an artist and illustrator and he also worked from home, so they were both on site to see to the donkeys.

They worked hard and very long hours. Erin helped out with the donkeys before and after school and at weekends. Charlie lived nearby in the village and came up to help out whenever he could.

They also had two voluntary helpers, Ralph, who was taking a year out from his studies before starting at veterinary school, and Emma who went to college locally and came as often as she could.

Mum and Dad were back, sitting in the kitchen, clutching cups of tea.

As soon as she walked in, Erin could tell there was something wrong. "What's happened?"

"Mr Benn didn't make a will," Mum told them. "And his nephew says he doesn't know anything about Mr Benn intending to leave the fields to us."

Erin couldn't believe what she was hearing. "But he's got to let us have the fields! Mr Benn promised. It's what he wanted!"

"We can't prove it," said Dad.

"But surely, if he's Mr Benn's nephew, he must know that he wanted to leave the land to the sanctuary," said Erin.

"Apparently not," said Mum. "Mr Benn obviously didn't expect to die so suddenly and he hadn't got round to making his will. So now his entire estate has gone to his only living relative – his nephew."

"But that's awful," cried Charlie. "What are you going to do?"

"Well, he did say he'd continue renting the fields out to us – for now," said Dad.

"But he also said it was hardly worth his while – for the amount he got out of it,"

Mum added. "Mr Benn only charged us a very low rent."

"He told us he's 'considering his options'," said Dad.

"Maybe he'll decide to just continue renting to you," Charlie suggested hopefully.

"But what if he doesn't?" cried Erin. "We've got twenty-five donkeys to look after. What are we going to do?"

No one had any answers.

Chapter 2

Amber

The next morning, Erin was still grooming Benedict when Charlie called for her for school.

"Almost finished," she told him. "I've groomed a couple of extra donkeys this morning to help Mum. Two of our guests got up late so she's still cooking their breakfast."

She brushed Benedict's shaggy forehead then led him over to the field. It was a dry and mild December, so thankfully the donkeys could still spend quite a bit of time out in the fields.

She quickly changed her coat, washed her hands and grabbed her school bag. Then with a quick wave to Dad, who was cleaning out the big barn, they set off for school. "Dad's going to talk to his solicitor today," Erin told Charlie. "To see if we've got any rights over the land."

"That's a good idea," said Charlie.

"They put all their savings into starting the sanctuary," said Erin. "And they work so hard to make sure the donkeys are well cared for."

"I know," said Charlie. "I'm sure they'll be able to sort something out."

Just down the road they met up with their friends Matthew, James and Hannah. Hannah was the younger sister of Emma, their helper. All three of them were interested in what was happening at the sanctuary.

Erin had just started to tell them about the possible problems when she spotted Amber Trueman, the new girl in their class, on the opposite side of the road.

"I haven't spoken to her yet," said Erin. "We'd better be friendly. Hey, Amber," she called to her. "You want to walk to school with us?"

Amber glanced over to them. Then she tossed back her long golden curls and, without a word, just carried on walking.

"I shouldn't bother with her," said Hannah. "She doesn't seem to want to make friends with anyone."

"I asked her where she lived yesterday," said Matthew. "She said it was none of my business and told me to get lost."

"Then she made Sarah cry at lunchtime," said James. "But Sarah wouldn't tell anyone what she'd said to her."

"And she's already been in trouble lots of times at school," said Hannah.

"Perhaps she's just feeling a bit strange," said Erin. "Being new and all that."

"Forget her," said Charlie. "We've got other things to worry about."

But it was difficult to forget Amber – she was in trouble again that morning for wearing a gold bracelet to school.

"You'll have to take it off," said Mr Reynolds, one of the teachers. "I'll put it in the safe – it looks very expensive."

"Of course it's expensive," Amber retorted. "My father always buys me expensive things and I'm not trusting you with it."

She refused to take it off.

"Right, then you leave me no choice," Mr Reynolds told her. "I'm sending you to the headmaster, and your father will be called in to take you home."

Erin and Charlie saw her leaving with him at lunchtime. "I can't believe it," he was saying to her. "You've hardly been here a week and I've been sent for. That's a record – even for you."

After school, Erin was anxious to find out how her father had got on with the solicitor but he was in his studio, working on some illustrations for a book. She found Mum in the big barn putting out the donkeys' evening hay.

"The news isn't good," she told Erin. "Because there was no will, and no written agreement with Mr Benn, we don't have any legal rights over the land."

"So he can just chuck us off if he wants to?" said Erin.

Mum nodded. "I'm afraid so."

They walked together in silence over to the main donkeys' field. The donkeys were all waiting by the gate – except Benedict who was standing alone with his head down as usual. The donkeys always seemed to know when it was time to go in – or as Dad said, it was more likely they knew it was suppertime!

Erin opened the large gate and waited as all the donkeys trotted over to the barn.

Benedict ambled through after them and headed for the far corner of the barn to eat his supper alone.

"Can't you try talking to this nephew of Mr Benn's again?" asked Erin.

"His name's Major Trueman. He's been in the army, but now he's a businessman of some sort," said Mum. "And yes, we are going to see him to try and persuade him to let us stay. But he said he's too busy to see us until Tuesday week."

"Major Trueman?" said Erin. There was something familiar about the name. "Amber Trueman!" He was Amber's father.

The following day was Saturday and Charlie came up to help Erin clean out the donkeys' barns. As they worked, she told him the latest developments.

"I thought we could talk to Amber about the sanctuary on Monday," said Erin. "Tell her all about it and see if we can get her on our side."

"You kidding?" said Charlie.

"Maybe she was just having a bad day yesterday," said Erin.

"More like a bad week," said Charlie.

Erin wasn't going to be put off. "I'll invite her over to meet the donkeys. She'll love them – everyone does."

They were just putting fresh straw in the senior barn when Mrs Moffatt, one of their teachers, arrived.

She was a familiar sight around the village with her map and her compass. All her spare time was spent searching for Roman remains.

"Hello, Mrs Moffatt," said Erin. "How are the ruins?"

Mrs Moffatt looked at the children over the top of her glasses. "Oh, my dears, there's such excitement." She clasped her hands together in delight. "The remains of a Roman villa have just been uncovered in a field at Horton. Imagine that – just three kilometres away."

"Wow! That's great," said Charlie.

"And with the Roman wall at the other end of this village, it's now certain that there was a Roman settlement right here. Plus," she pushed her glasses to the top of her nose and her grey eyes twinkled through them, "from the pottery we've dug up round here recently there has to be a bathhouse very close by."

"Well, I hope you find it soon," said Erin.

"I'm sure we will," said the teacher. "Anyway, what I came for was to ask your parents if I can borrow a donkey."

"Borrow a donkey?" said Charlie.

"Yes, I'm putting on a nativity play with your class and I thought it would be lovely to have a real donkey," Mrs Moffatt explained.

"That's a brilliant idea," said Erin. "A school at Horton borrowed one for their nativity last year and it was a great success. I'm sure Mum and Dad will agree."

"Oh good." Mrs Moffatt beamed at them. "And you two are going to be lovely angels."

Charlie opened his mouth to protest and Erin stifled a laugh.

"Before you say anything, Charlie dear, I do know you're a boy," said Mrs Moffatt. "You're going to be the Angel Gabriel."

Charlie laughed. "Oh, right."

Then she left them to get on and went off to speak to Erin's parents.

Erin and Charlie spent most of Sunday trying to cheer Benedict up. Charlie produced a green floppy hat and put it on. But Benedict ignored him as usual. No amount of fuss they made of him made any difference at all.

"Poor Benedict," said Erin. "Are you really expecting to be moved on again soon?"

"That's exactly what will happen if Major Trueman doesn't let you stay," said Charlie.

"I know." Erin scratched Benedict on his shaggy head between his ears. "It makes it all the more important to talk to Amber. We've got to get her to convince her father that the donkeys need to stay on their land."

"Well, I suppose it has to be worth a try," said Charlie.

Chapter 3

Angels

Erin and Charlie caught Amber up on the way to school on Monday. Hannah, Matthew and James were with them and helped persuade Amber to stop and listen. She scowled and looked down at the pavement as Erin started to explain about the work of the donkey sanctuary.

"We've already helped so many donkeys in distress," she told her. "You won't believe what's happened to some of them. What terrible lives they've had."

Amber listened to them silently, but kept staring at the pavement.

"And there's lots more that need help," Charlie joined in.

"So I wondered if you'd like to come and meet them," said Erin. "And then maybe you could—"

Amber suddenly looked up. "Why would I want to meet moth-eaten, smelly donkeys?" she said. "I can see them from my window – and hear them when I'm in the garden. That awful noise they make."

Erin was completely taken aback. "They're not moth-eaten – or smelly – we keep them clean. And they hardly ever make a noise! And it's not awful – they're just talking." She took a deep breath and tried desperately to keep her temper. "Look, I'm sure if you just came—"

"No I won't," said Amber. "I hate them." She pushed past Matthew and James and strode off.

Erin's green eyes flashed as she watched her walk off. Then she turned to Charlie. "Don't you dare say 'I told you so'."

"Well – she's certainly not going to put in a good word for you with her father," said Hannah.

"He probably wouldn't listen to her anyway," said Matthew. "Not when it's business."

"Well, now we know how she feels, let's hope he doesn't," said James.

Erin found it difficult to concentrate on any school work all day. For the last lesson, the class gathered in the hall for the casting of the nativity play. Mrs Moffatt bustled about in her usual enthusiastic way clutching a list and a pile of scripts. She cast Hannah as Mary and Winston as Joseph. Matthew and James were two of the shepherds.

"Now, Charlie is the Angel Gabriel and Erin is another angel," she said, looking up

over her glasses. "We just need one more."
She consulted her list again. "Ah yes, Amber."

"Oh no!" Erin whispered. "I don't believe it."

"She's the least like an angel in the whole class," whispered Matthew.

Amber wasn't pleased either. She sat bolt upright and folded her arms. "I don't want to be an angel. I don't want to be in it at all."

"Sorry, Amber, but everyone will be taking part," said Mrs Moffatt.

Amber looked at her sulkily. "Yes – but an angel? Couldn't I be something else? An innkeeper maybe – the one that turns Mary and Joseph away – I could be really mean."

"That's not hard to imagine," whispered Charlie.

"No, dear, we've got all the innkeepers we need," said Mrs Moffatt. "And you'll make a lovely angel – with all that golden hair."

"Huh!" Amber slumped back down in her seat.

"You know, she'd be quite pretty – if she didn't scowl so much," whispered Hannah.

Then Mrs Moffatt announced that she had a surprise for them. "This is going to be a really special nativity play, children. We're going to have a real live donkey in it."

The children were all thrilled – except Amber. "That's disgusting," she complained.

"You can't bring one of those smelly creatures in here."

"Amber, there is no reason why we can't use a real donkey," said Mrs Moffatt. "They certainly don't smell and all the necessary arrangements have been made."

"Yeah, and we all want a real donkey," said Matthew.

The bell went for the end of school and Amber pushed past everyone as they left the hall. "I suppose all your mummies and daddies will be coming to watch their little diddums in the nativity play," she sneered.

"Won't yours?" asked Winston.

"No," said Amber very definitely, and walked on ahead of them.

"What about her mum?" asked James.

Hannah shrugged. "Dunno. She never mentions anything about her family. Except that her father buys her expensive presents all the time."

Erin and Charlie arrived back at the sanctuary to see Emma leading Cherie across the yard.

They went over to make a fuss of her. Erin gently rubbed the pretty little brown and white donkey's nose. "Is Cherie about to give birth?" she asked Emma.

"We can't be sure," she said. "It's always difficult to tell with a donkey, and we don't even know when Cherie got pregnant. But your mum thinks it could be very soon so we're keeping an eye on her."

"She looks great, doesn't she?" said Charlie. "When you think what she looked like when you picked her up."

Cherie had been found abandoned in some woods. She was very frightened and too nervous to allow anyone to go near her. It had taken some time to win her trust and, when the vet had examined her, he'd found her to be pregnant. She'd also been very thin and the vet was worried that all her nourishment had gone to the growing foal inside her.

"Yes, she's looking good now, but she still needs lots of tender loving care," said Emma. "Don't you, girl?" She ruffled Cherie's spiky mane. "Lots of TLC."

The little donkey looked up at her with soft trusting eyes.

Erin and Charlie dumped their school bags and put on old coats. Then they each fetched a head collar and lead and went over to the donkeys' field.

Lucy-May, a light-brown donkey with a white tummy, was in the field for the first time. They watched her investigating every corner of it. All the donkeys (apart from Benedict who had shown no interest) did this when introduced to a new environment.

Erin went over to Benedict and the little donkey just stood still while she put the head collar on him. But he showed no sign of acknowledging her.

Charlie put a head collar on Joseph. He had a beautiful "many coloured" coat and had arrived at the sanctuary without a name, so they'd called him Joseph, after Joseph and his coat of many colours in the Bible story.

They led the two donkeys across the field and into the yard.

Erin picked up two hoof picks and handed one to Charlie. She reached down and touched Benedict's foot and he immediately lifted it for her. "Good boy," said Erin, as she started to pick the mud out of his hoof. "You're so easy to handle, aren't you?"

"If only we could cheer him up," said Charlie.

"Hey," said Erin. "I've just had a brilliant idea."

"You have?" Charlie looked up from cleaning Joseph's front hoof.

"Yes. It's not just you who gets bright ideas," said Erin. "I can have them too."

"OK," grinned Charlie. "What's this brilliant idea?"

"We use Benedict in the nativity play," said Erin. "He's so easy to handle and all the kids are bound to make a fuss of him. It might cheer him up."

"That's such a great idea, I could have thought of it myself," said Charlie.

"I'm sure Mum and Dad will agree," said Erin. "And it's really important we get him used to people – just in case – you know..."

"You get chucked off the land and he has to be rehomed again," Charlie finished for her.

Chapter 4

The Christmas Wish

Mum and Dad thought it could be very good for Benedict to appear in the nativity play and Ralph offered to walk him down for rehearsals.

"We've been doing a lot of thinking," said Dad. "And we've decided that when we have our meeting with Major Trueman next Tuesday, we're going to offer to pay him more rent. Hopefully it will encourage him to let the sanctuary stay when he gets round to 'considering his options'."

"But how?" asked Erin. She knew that money was always tight. The cost of caring for twenty-five donkeys was pretty high. They did get donations from the public but every penny was used up.

"I've been to see a new art dealer today," said Dad. "He's taken several of my paintings to display at his London gallery and if they attract interest over the weekend he'll take more on a regular basis."

"And we thought we could sell Christmas cards and calendars made from prints of some of your dad's donkey paintings," said Mum.

"That's great," said Erin.

"What about getting people to adopt a donkey?" Charlie suggested. "The donkey still stays here, of course, but each person would pay you some money every year towards its keep. You give them an adoption certificate, and a photo, and maybe information on their donkey. And send them news every so often."

"Brilliant," said Erin. "And you and I could run it, Charlie, couldn't we?"

Mum and Dad thought this was a good idea too. Children from school might be interested – particularly after seeing Benedict in the nativity play. And there were always lots of visitors to the sanctuary, especially in the summer, who might be keen to adopt a donkey.

Hopefully Dad would get a good response from the art dealer on Monday. If so, then they would be in a good position to make Major Trueman an offer on the rent next Tuesday.

At school the next day, they gathered for a rehearsal of the nativity play.

But first Mrs Moffatt handed everyone a star. "I'm going to stick these on a dark blue backcloth to represent the night sky for the play," she told them. "But first, I want you all to think of a Christmas wish – a special wish for this special time of year," she said. "Something thoughtful and loving for others. Then I want you to write just a word or two on your star to remind you of your wish."

Erin didn't need to stop and think. She desperately wished that Benedict and the other donkeys could stay on their land to be loved and well cared for. She carefully wrote "Donkeys" on her star.

Charlie did the same. Others wrote things that were important to them, the name of a sick aunt, a lost cat, a day centre... Amber wrote "big expensive house" and got told off because that was selfish. So she crossed it out and reluctantly scribbled "poor people".

"Now we're just going to walk through the play today," Mrs Moffatt told them. "We'll have a proper rehearsal tomorrow and another one on Thursday. Then on Friday we should be ready to bring the donkey in."

She told them that the play was going to be performed on the last day of term. It was just three weeks away, so they had to get on with learning their lines.

The first two rehearsals went really well, but everyone was waiting for the donkey to arrive – everyone except Amber. When the children arrived for the rehearsal on Friday afternoon, they found that the hall had been decorated and a huge Christmas tree put up.

The "night sky" backcloth was in place at the back of the stage. The children's stars surrounded the large Star of Bethlehem. Erin smiled as she looked up and spotted her wish.

Then Ralph arrived with Benedict. He carefully spread straw all over the stage for the little donkey to stand on. All the children (apart from Amber) were keen to stroke and pat him. Ralph organized them to come up to him in twos so they didn't frighten him. But the little donkey just stood there. Being made a fuss of by so many children had no effect on him at all.

Ralph suggested that Benedict should get used to being there first of all so he led him over to the side of the stage to watch.

Amber was sitting on her own, slumped in the corner. "I don't see why we have to have a real donkey," she complained, holding her nose. "Why can't we have a toy one on wheels or something? It's not as if we've got real lambs, is it? The shepherds are holding crummy knitted ones."

"You don't get lambs in December in this country, Amber," said Mrs Moffatt patiently. "And it makes it special to have a real donkey. Especially as the donkeys are very much a part of the village life."

Amber gave a sly look over to Erin. "Wanna bet?" she muttered.

Erin jumped to her feet, her green eyes flashing.

"She's just winding you up," said Charlie.

"Now calm down, everyone," said Mrs Moffatt. "Let's get on with it."

Under the teacher's enthusiastic guidance, Mary and Joseph knocked on the innkeepers' doors, finally ending up in the stable. Then the three angels appeared to the shepherds who were watching their flocks.

Benedict just stood there taking no notice of anything at all. He could still have been in his field for all the effect it was having on him. Even when one of the three kings tripped over right in front of him he didn't flinch.

Amber continued to sulk. Any time she wasn't needed she slid away to stand or sit on her own, scowling.

The rehearsal was just finished when she started complaining again. "Why's he watching me?"

They all looked up to see what she was talking about. No one had been watching her. They were all concentrating on what they were doing. Then Erin's eyes strayed to Benedict. He'd actually raised his head –

and there was no doubt about it. He was watching Amber!

"I expect he's thinking what a pretty angel you're going to be," said Mrs Moffatt.

"Huh!" said Amber. "Just tell him to stop looking at me."

Erin was amazed – and cross. "The first time he's shown any sign of reacting to anyone," she complained to Charlie, as they left the hall. "And he has to pick Amber Trueman!"

"And I thought that donkeys were supposed to be intelligent," said Charlie.

Chapter 5

Some Angel!

On Saturday, Erin and Charlie made an early start. As soon as they'd helped groom the donkeys, they started on the adoption scheme. They designed adoption certificates on the computer and ran them off ready to fill in with the names.

Then on Sunday, after they'd helped Dad put up the Christmas lights on the two big fir trees at the entrance, they borrowed his digital camera to take pictures of the donkeys.

John, Paul, George and Ringo seemed very keen to have their photos taken and posed beautifully.

"I'm sure Ringo just fluttered his eyelashes at me," Charlie joked.

"They must have got used to posing for pictures when they were beach donkeys," said Erin.

Arthur and Clover didn't like being separated for their photos. Arthur kept looking behind him for Clover, and Clover got quite upset when she was held back from Arthur.

"They'll just have to be together," said Erin. "We can charge a special rate for Arthur and Clover as a pair."

They made a lovely photo with the lit-up fir trees in the background. "Just like an old married couple," said Charlie.

They tried hard to get a photo of Benedict that didn't make him look too sad. "Come on, Benedict," said Erin softly.

"Look up. Just for a minute. If we get people to adopt you, they'll come and visit you and maybe cheer you up."

In the end they just had to take his photo as he was. "You never know, it might actually work in his favour," said Charlie. "People might want to adopt him because they feel sorry for him."

Over in the senior field, Peanut was fascinated by the camera. He kept coming right up to it and putting his nose on the lens. "Hey, you're misting it all up," laughed Charlie.

"I just know we're going to raise lots of money with this," said Erin.

"Course we are," said Charlie. "And let's hope your dad gets some good news from the art dealer tomorrow."

On Monday morning they had another rehearsal for the nativity play. As soon as Ralph arrived with Benedict, the little donkey spotted Amber. She was standing on her own as usual, scowling at everyone.

"He's watching me again," she complained.

"He probably can't believe how awful she is," whispered Matthew.

"Now, we don't want any arguments today," said Mrs Moffatt.

Benedict didn't take his eyes off Amber once during the rehearsal. Even when she went and stood right in the far corner, his soft dark eyes followed her.

When it came to the nativity scene Mrs Moffatt decided it was time to get Benedict involved.

"We'll have the Angel Gabriel standing over here to the left of the manger," she said. "That's right, Charlie. Then we'll have Amber kneeling on your right. Come on now, Amber dear, and do stop scowling."

Erin was to kneel on Charlie's left and Mrs Moffatt asked her to walk Benedict over and let him stand by her side so she could keep an eye on him. "Mary and Joseph, come and sit behind the manger, and don't forget Baby Jesus." Hannah carefully picked up the doll wrapped in a white blanket.

Benedict walked obediently with Erin and stood in his place between her and the manger. "Oh, this is going to be so lovely," cried Mrs Moffatt.

But Benedict suddenly decided to make a move. As quick as a flash he dodged behind Erin and Charlie and nudged Amber gently in the back with his nose.

She was on her feet in seconds. "He attacked me!"

"Don't be ridiculous!" Erin jumped up to grab Benedict's reins. "He's only trying to get your attention."

Amber stamped off over to the corner and slumped down.

Benedict watched her go. His gentle eyes looked puzzled. Erin threw her arms round his neck. "Don't worry about her," she whispered. "She doesn't realize how lucky she is that you've chosen her."

"Lucky?" shrieked Amber. "What's lucky about being bashed by a smelly donkey?"

"He's not smelly – and he didn't bash you, he just wanted to play."

"Now come on, angels," said Mrs Moffatt. She hastily pushed her glasses to the top of her nose and looked unusually stern. "Back into your places."

Amber reluctantly shuffled over.

"Erin, you'll have to keep hold of Benedict for the time being," said Mrs Moffatt.

"Just keep him away from me," said Amber.

Erin glared at her. *Some angel*, she thought. But then she wasn't exactly having angelic thoughts about Amber herself!

"What's the matter with that donkey?" whispered Charlie. "All the other children love him – but what does he do? He chooses Amber Trueman to make friends with!"

"I haven't got a clue," said Erin. "She'll probably go home and complain to her father – and that's not exactly going to help our cause, is it?"

She kissed the little donkey on his soft nose. "Oh, Benedict."

After school, Erin arrived back at the sanctuary to see Emma leading Fred down the ramp from the trailer. Once a month she helped Mum take Fred and Tapestry to a school for special needs children.

Erin waved to her. "Hi Emma. How did it go at the school today?"

"Great," said Emma. "And Fred's been such a good boy, haven't you, Fred?" She led the little grey donkey with a white face towards the field. "You should see the looks on those kids' faces when the donkeys arrive," she told Erin. "There was one little boy today that couldn't walk, but we held him up on Fred's back and he just loved it. His little face was a picture."

Erin smiled at her. Emma was so good with the donkeys and with the children too. Mum was hoping to extend their visits to other schools very soon.

Mum started leading Tapestry down the

ramp. Tapestry was a beautiful skewbald mare and, like Fred, was a particularly gentle donkey. The two donkeys seemed to enjoy their visits to the school as much as the children did.

"I've got some good news," called Mum. "The art dealer's phoned and he's sold two of Dad's paintings. He wants him to supply him on a regular basis now."

"Wow! That's great," said Erin.

"It certainly is," said Mum. "Now we're in a good position to offer more rent to Major Trueman when we see him tomorrow."

She led Tapestry into the field and the little donkey trotted off to join the others. Emma was chatting to Benedict. She was also trying to help him settle by spending as much time with him as she could.

Erin watched them all. "Fingers crossed for tomorrow then," she said.

Chapter 6

Hope

At school, the following day, the rehearsal for the nativity play went well. Benedict watched Amber – and Amber watched Benedict to make sure he didn't come near her.

They finished early to start sorting out the costumes.

Ralph set about clearing up some of the straw while Mrs Moffatt gleefully dressed up Mary and Joseph. Benedict was obediently standing behind the curtain at the side of the stage.

Mrs Moffatt moved on to the three angels. Charlie and Erin were soon fitted out and Amber had her white robe and a pair of wings.

"Now I just need a halo for Amber," she said, looking behind her.

"A halo?" joked one of the innkeepers. "A pair of horns would be more like it!"

"We'll have none of that talk," said Mrs Moffatt, placing the halo firmly on Amber's head.

Amber was furious and rushed across the stage to the offending innkeeper. "You mindless moron –" she started. Then she stopped and looked puzzled for a minute. In her fury, she'd forgotten to take note of where Benedict was. He'd come out from behind the curtain and was now behind her, gently nudging at her halo.

Amber cringed and brought her hands up to her face. "Get off. Get him off!"

With an expert flick of his head, Benedict

whipped the halo right off her head.

Everyone laughed. "See, the donkey doesn't think she should have a halo either," said James.

Benedict tossed his head with his prize. The more everyone laughed, the more furious Amber got.

Once again, Mrs Moffatt calmed everyone down. Ralph took the halo from Benedict and handed it back to Amber.

"I'm not wearing that!" she exclaimed. "Not now that donkey-breath has had it in his mouth."

"He's only playing," said Erin. She took her own halo off and handed it to Amber. "Here, I'll wear yours."

Amber took it and threw it on the ground. "I don't want to be an angel."

"I must admit you're proving to be a bit miscast," said Mrs Moffatt. "But there's no time to change now."

Erin was relieved when it was finally home time. She and Charlie rushed back to the sanctuary eager to find out how the meeting with Major Trueman had gone.

Ralph had just got back with Benedict. "Your parents are in the isolation unit seeing to a new donkey that's just come in," he told Erin.

Erin put her head round the door. She knew immediately by their faces that the meeting with Major Trueman hadn't gone well.

"What's happened? Wasn't the rent you offered high enough?"

Dad gently stroked the thick fur of the little black donkey. "Let's go outside," he whispered. "Give him a chance to settle. He's a bit anxious."

Mum quietly closed the door behind them. "I'm afraid Major Trueman wasn't interested in the increased rent," she told Erin. "He said it still amounted to almost nothing."

Then Dad dropped the bombshell. "He's decided to sell the land."

"But why?" cried Erin. "I mean – he can't!"

"I'm afraid he can – it's legally his land," said Dad bitterly. "He's asking £250,000 for the two fields and the wooded area next to them."

"What?"

"Apparently it's not just grazing land, as we thought," said Mum. "Major Trueman's made enquiries and it's prime development land. That's why the price is so high."

"There's no way we can raise that sort of money," said Dad. "So he's given us, what he considers to be 'fair warning' to start looking for other fields."

"He's got no idea that we can't just rent fields elsewhere," said Mum. "We've got to live at the sanctuary. The donkeys need twenty-four-hour supervision."

"And it's very unlikely that we can afford to move," said Dad. "We need a house big enough to run the bed and breakfast, as that's the main income for the sanctuary. And a new house with enough land for the donkeys to live on as well will be just too expensive."

"But you will look, won't you?" cried Erin. "There must be somewhere…"

Dad nodded. "I've already been on to a couple of estate agents. I don't hold out much hope – but we'll certainly try all we can."

"Maybe we could get Major Trueman to change his mind." said Charlie. "We know that most of the people in the village love the donkeys, so why don't we organize a petition?"

Erin was enthusiastic. "Yes – come on, it's got to be worth a try."

"Well, you can try if you want to," said Dad. "But I'm afraid I don't really hold out much hope of changing his mind."

It was already dusk when they went to get the rest of the donkeys in for the night. Across the fields, Erin could see lights on in the Truemans' house. Upstairs, a shadowy figure was looking out over the donkeys' fields. She guessed it was Amber.

That's one person who will be pleased to see the donkeys go, thought Erin.

Erin didn't expect to sleep much that night – and she didn't. She was still awake when the donkeys started braying at two o'clock in the morning. She sat bolt upright. Something was wrong. The donkeys didn't usually bray at night.

Mum and Dad were already pulling on their coats and boots when she got downstairs. They rushed out into the cold December night and over to the main barn.

It was obvious as soon as they opened the door what the trouble was. Cherie was about to give birth to her foal.

"It never fails to amaze me, the way the donkeys let us know when we're needed," said Mum. "They're such incredible creatures."

She'd been very concerned about Cherie, as she'd been so thin when they'd taken her in. But as it happened she needn't have worried. Within the hour, and without needing any assistance, Cherie had given birth to a tiny, but perfect, foal.

"It's a girl – a Jenny donkey," said Dad. They watched as the tiny creature struggled to stand up straight away. "And she looks just like her mum."

Tears streamed down Erin's face as she watched Cherie licking the tiny bundle of wet fur. She'd seen foals born before and it was always wonderful – but this one seemed special.

"Let's call her Hope," she suggested.

Chapter 7

The Petition

The next morning, Charlie came round early. He was thrilled to see Hope and thought it was a great name. He'd already drawn up pages for the petition which asked people to sign in support of the donkey sanctuary staying on the land.

Erin was very tired – she'd finally dropped off to sleep around four o'clock. But the birth of little Hope had given her just that, a tiny spark of hope that, just maybe, things might turn out all right.

As soon as they reached the school playground, they started collecting signatures on the petition. All the children they asked wanted to sign plus a couple of teachers they caught on their way in. But when Amber saw what they were up to she looked really angry.

"Why would anybody be interested in keeping a load of smelly donkeys?" she declared in a loud voice. "And has anyone noticed?" she called across the playground, in an even louder voice. "That Erin is beginning to smell like a donkey?"

"Just ignore her," said Charlie.

"No one's going to believe her," said Hannah.

But when a girl came up behind Erin and actually sniffed, she lost her cool. "She's lying! OK?" she shouted at the surprised girl. "She's lying!" she screamed at the playground in general.

"I think they've got the message," said Matthew.

After lunch, they had a rehearsal for the nativity play. Benedict trotted in with Ralph and immediately looked round the hall for Amber. Amber concentrated on keeping well out of his way and Erin tried to distract him by talking to him whenever she could. Charlie, Hannah, Matthew and James also took turns in making a fuss of him. But Benedict didn't respond, he just wanted to watch Amber all the time.

Erin kept a tight rein on him and the rehearsal actually went well.

Just before they left for home Mrs Moffatt produced a camera. "I'm going to take a lovely photo for the school newsletter," she told them.

She called Charlie and Amber over and asked Erin to bring Benedict. "Three Christmas Angels – and a donkey," she said. "That will make a lovely picture!"

That reminded Erin that it could be the last Christmas for the donkey sanctuary. Charlie must have been thinking the same by the look on his face.

They made an unusual group. Two worried-looking angels, one scowling angel, and a donkey that seemed more interested in looking at the scowling angel than at the camera.

"Do try and smile," said Mrs Moffatt. Then, just as she clicked the camera, Benedict suddenly reached over and whipped Amber's halo off.

Everyone laughed but to their surprise, Amber burst into tears. "Don't you dare put that picture in your rotten newsletter," she shouted at Mrs Moffatt. "Erin set that donkey on me on purpose."

"Of course I didn't, stupid," said Erin. "For some totally weird reason he likes you."

Amber stopped sobbing for a moment and glared at her. She opened her mouth to retort but then the bell went for home time and Mrs Moffatt hastily started ushering them all out.

"I want to get home in good time tonight," she told them. "My archaeological society has arranged a dig over at Borden Grange. One of our members thinks the Roman bathhouse could be somewhere near there."

Amber watched her scurry past. "She's batty," she said to no one in particular.

Over the next three days, Hannah, Matthew and James helped Erin and Charlie collect signatures on the petition. They took copies into local shops and asked everyone they knew. Dad took a copy into the local pub and all the visitors to the sanctuary signed it.

On Saturday evening, Erin and Charlie sat down to gather all the pages together. They had to clear the kitchen table of newspapers first. Erin's parents had been scanning the advertisements in every newspaper they could get hold of for a large, cheap house with its own land. But they'd found nothing. They'd also put their own adverts in all the papers asking if anyone had suitable premises they were thinking of selling. But so far no one had even phoned.

Erin was pleased with the petition when they put all the pages together. "We've got the support of most of the village," she said.

She picked up a folder to put it in and found it was the one with all the donkeys' photos for the adoption scheme in. She sighed. "If the petition doesn't convince Major Trueman to change his mind then we won't be needing these."

"Hey, that's given me an idea," said Charlie. "When we take the petition to Major Trueman, let's show him some of the photos and you can tell him the donkeys' stories."

"Brilliant," said Erin. "And I'll get some of the photos Dad's taken when the donkeys first came in. Before and after photos – so he can see for himself the sort of work we're doing here."

"He won't be able to resist," said Charlie.

On Sunday morning, armed with the petition and the donkeys' photos, Erin and Charlie nervously made their way to the Truemans' house.

Amber answered the door. "What do you want?"

"To see your father," said Charlie.

"He doesn't see anyone without an appointment," said Amber. "And he certainly doesn't want to see you."

Just then Major Trueman appeared at the door. "Let them in, Amber. It's cold with the door open."

Amber looked cross. "All right. But take

off your shoes – and leave them outside," she said, holding her nose. "We don't want disgusting donkey muck in here."

They followed her into a comfortable living room and Major Trueman invited them to sit down. Amber slumped into a chair and started flicking noisily through a magazine.

The major looked at the petition and at the photos they showed him. He listened carefully without interrupting as Erin told him some of the donkeys' stories.

Then patiently and very politely he explained that he just didn't share their passion for donkeys. "I don't doubt that you are doing something useful – and that you have the support of some of the village. But now that you've got these donkeys on their feet again, they can be looked after elsewhere."

"But there are loads more that need help – and a good home," Erin cried.

"Then they'll have to be looked after elsewhere too," said Major Trueman. "The land belongs to me and I can see no reason why I shouldn't sell it. If you're bored then I'm sure you can find something else to do."

"Bored?" Erin's green eyes flashed. She thought she might explode. "It's nothing to do with being bored."

"There's nowhere else round here for donkeys to be helped and looked after," Charlie explained. "That's why Erin's parents took them in, in the first place."

"I'm sorry but it's not my concern," said the major.

Erin stared at him. For once she was speechless. The only sound in the room was Amber still flicking noisily through her magazine.

Then Charlie touched Erin's arm. "Come on, Erin, we're wasting our time here."

Erin grabbed the photos and stamped over to the door, scattering the pages of the petition as she went.

Chapter 8

The Carrot Theft

At school on Monday, Erin was surprised when Amber totally ignored her. She was sure she'd been listening yesterday – and just pretending she wasn't interested by flicking through the magazine. She'd expected her to be triumphant – jeering. But she seemed to be concentrating on being even more badly behaved than usual.

She tore up Hannah's homework, swore at Mrs Moffatt, threw the ball over the fence in games and pushed two younger children over in the playground.

Eventually, her father was called in to take her home. She was warned that if she didn't change her ways she risked being suspended from school.

"That would be a relief," said Matthew.

There was no rehearsal for the nativity play that day so Benedict was in the field when Erin got home. He was across the other side by the fence and a hooded figure was leaning over it talking to him. It was obviously Emma, having one of her chats with him before putting the donkeys away for the night.

"Hi, Emma," she called. The figure seemed to hesitate, then waved without looking round.

Mum and Dad were with the older donkeys in the senior barn. Mum was measuring out some pony nuts for them, closely watched by Whisky, who always enjoyed her food. Dad was checking their rugs, followed by Peanut, who liked to oversee everything that went on in his barn. "I don't think you'll manage to pull these rugs off," he told him, ruffling his shaggy coat. "I've made them nice and secure."

Sybil and Candy's heads were intertwined, grooming each other's backs, and Pepe was just trotting in from the field.

When Erin had told her parents last night that the petition hadn't worked, Mum had smiled and thanked them for trying. But she knew Mum was just putting on a brave face about it.

Now she looked tearful and Dad's face was very strained.

"We've been in touch with every estate agent around now," said Dad. "But for what we need, it's all much too expensive. I'm afraid things aren't looking very optimistic."

Erin was close to tears herself. She couldn't imagine life without the donkeys. "But we're not giving up yet, are we?"

"No, but we have managed to find somewhere that will take the five older donkeys – just in case," Mum told her. "We're still looking for good homes for the other twenty-two."

"I blame myself," said Dad. "I should have sorted something more permanent out long ago."

"But you weren't to know that Mr Benn was going to die suddenly," said Erin. "Or that he hadn't made out his will."

"Maybe not," said Dad. "But even so..."

"You can't blame yourself," said Mum.

"Now come on, we'd better get the other donkeys in."

"It's all right. Emma's doing it," said Erin.

"No, Emma's not here today. She had to go into college about her new course," said Mum.

"Then who's that out there with Benedict?"

They rushed outside but the person was gone.

"Probably just one of the visitors," said Dad. "We've had quite a few today. I thought they'd all left when I shut the gate."

Benedict was OK, so they got on with putting the supper in the big barn, ready for bringing the donkeys in.

The next day at school, Amber was surprisingly well behaved – obviously yesterday's threat of being suspended had worked.

There was a rehearsal for the nativity

play in the morning. Ralph had brought Benedict in, but now he was busy dragging another straw bale up on to the stage. Then as Erin also turned away, to look up at her star, Benedict seized his chance to get over to Amber.

She gave a little cry as he nudged her from behind but she didn't say a word. Erin watched in disbelief as Amber just closed her eyes for a second and then stepped away from him.

Erin grabbed Benedict's rein and led the little donkey away. "D'you reckon Amber's really changed that much?" she whispered to Charlie. "Just overnight?"

Charlie shook his head. "Can't have. She's up to something."

The rehearsal was going well and they'd just got to the arrival of the three kings when the headmaster came in. "I'm sorry to interrupt, Mrs Moffatt, but it appears that a number of carrots have been stolen from the school kitchens," he announced. "And I rather suspect that someone in this class has something to do with it."

Mrs Moffatt peered at the headmaster over the top of her glasses. "What makes you think my class has anything to do with it?"

The headmaster glanced at Benedict. "This class is the only one with a donkey in it."

Erin felt the anger rising in her. "Benedict hasn't been anywhere near the kitchens." She put her hand protectively on the donkey's shaggy neck.

The headmaster raised his eyes to the top of his head. "I didn't think that the donkey had stolen them. What I suspect is that one of you children took them to give to him."

They all looked round at each other. Most of the children shook their heads, and Erin explained indignantly that she wouldn't need to steal carrots as they had plenty at the sanctuary.

Amber just sat there looking innocent.

Too innocent, thought Erin. "Look at her – she looks like the perfect little angel," she whispered to Charlie. "I think you're right, she is up to something."

Erin thought back over the last few days. Amber had been sent home early yesterday. There was a mysterious hooded figure with Benedict when they got home. Now some carrots had been stolen. "I bet she's the carrot thief."

"But she wouldn't steal carrots to give to Benedict," said Charlie. "She hates him – she hates all donkeys."

"Maybe she wants the carrots to lure him over to her." A sudden chill shot up Erin's spine. "You don't suppose she'd hurt him, do you? Or even use them to poison him?"

"She couldn't get hold of any poison – and surely even Amber wouldn't..." started Charlie.

"Well, I don't trust her," said Erin. "She's up to something and we need to find out what it is."

"OK, let's set a trap for her after school," said Charlie. "Set her up so she thinks she's alone with Benedict."

"But we'll be watching her, right?" said Erin.

Charlie nodded.

Mrs Moffatt was still protesting the innocence of her class to the headmaster so Erin quickly went over to Ralph. "I can't explain now," she said. "But can you make sure Benedict is over by the woods when we get back from school. And can you be handy, but out of sight, in case we need you?"

Ralph looked puzzled but he agreed.

After school, Erin and Charlie got out of the gate before Amber. When they saw her coming they started talking loudly to Hannah, Matthew and James.

"We're not going straight to the sanctuary tonight," said Charlie.

"No, we're meeting my parents at the new out-of-town supermarket to help them with the shopping," said Erin.

Amber rushed straight past them clutching her suspiciously bulging school bag.

Erin and Charlie waited until she was out of sight. Then they raced across the fields towards the sanctuary and made their way through the woods to the donkeys' field. Benedict was standing just on the other side of the fence where Ralph had positioned him.

They quickly hid themselves behind a large bramble bush.

It wasn't long before they saw a figure coming across the field.

"It's her!" hissed Erin.

Chapter 9

Answers

Amber didn't need carrots to lure Benedict over. He looked up eagerly and trotted towards her.

"Hello, Benedict," said Amber.

Erin got ready to pounce.

But Amber brought up her hand and gently stroked the donkey's shaggy head. "You're such a clever little donkey, aren't you?" she said softly.

Benedict gave her a nudge with his nose and she giggled and stroked him again.

Erin and Charlie looked at each other in amazement.

"I don't know how, but you understand me, don't you?" said Amber. She took out a carrot and broke the end off. Benedict gently took it from her.

"I can't believe it – but you actually like me," she said. "No one else does."

She broke off another piece of carrot. "Oh, Dad buys me lots of expensive presents – but he's never got any time for me. Sometimes I think he wouldn't even notice if I wasn't there."

Erin and Charlie listened in silence as Amber continued to tell Benedict her story. Her mother had left when she was small and she hadn't seen her since. There'd been a series of au pairs to look after her, but none of them had stayed long. And they'd never kept in touch.

"Mind you, I wasn't always very nice to them." Amber scratched Benedict between his ears and he rubbed his head against her arm. Then she went on to say that her father had always been in the army. It meant that they'd moved around a lot. They'd never been in one place long enough for her to make good or lasting friends.

"Now no one likes me because I'm so nasty," she said. "But if they don't like me to start with then I know where I stand. I won't get fond of them and have to leave them – or have them leave me." She gave him another piece of carrot. "At least this way I can't get hurt any more."

Charlie shifted as he watched and Erin put her hand out to keep him still. She couldn't believe what she was hearing. Amber had never talked about herself to anyone. In fact, the only time she ever spoke at all was to complain or to be rude to someone.

Benedict was watching Amber intently. "You understood me right from the start, didn't you?" she said to him. "You're so wise – and so beautiful."

She gave him the last piece of carrot. "I'm sorry I didn't like you at first – I wasn't very nice to you, was I? But you didn't give up on me, like everyone else." She gently rubbed his soft nose. "But now – I-I don't know what's going to happen..."

She turned to leave. Benedict started to follow her across the field.

Erin and Charlie didn't need to discuss it. They quickly clambered over the fence and caught up with Amber.

"We just heard everything you said to Benedict," Charlie told her.

"You what?" Amber turned on them, furious. "How dare you spy on me?"

"We had to find out what you were up to," said Erin. "We thought you might hurt Benedict."

"Of course I wouldn't hurt Benedict," shouted Amber. "You're so stupid! You – you've got no idea what it's like being me."

"We've got more idea now," said Charlie. "At least now we know why you're so nasty to everyone."

Benedict came up and gave Amber a gentle push with his nose. She looked a bit embarrassed but she stroked him.

"He's never reacted to anyone here except you," Erin explained. "You're the only person he's put his trust in."

"I-I am?" said Amber. "W-why? Why me?"

"We wondered that too," said Charlie. "But your little conversation just now has explained a lot."

"He's been moved around lots of different homes," Erin explained. "Like you, he's never been allowed to really settle anywhere."

"And he must have been separated from donkey friends and people he'd got fond of in the past," said Charlie. "So he feels hurt and let down, just like you do. He won't let himself get fond of anyone in case he gets hurt again."

"That is, until he met you," said Erin.

"Are you saying that he actually spotted that in me?" said Amber. "That we have something in common?"

Erin nodded. "Donkeys are really intelligent."

They looked up and saw that Arthur, followed by Clover, had come to see what was going on. John, Paul, George and Ringo were watching from a little way away, with Joseph and Lucy-May. Fred and Tapestry were also on their way over with Chocolate.

Erin told Amber each of their names and explained how Chocolate had come to them as a tiny foal when his mother had died. They'd kept him in the warmth of their kitchen for quite a while and taken it in turns to bottle-feed him every couple of hours. He was now a handsome two year old.

"Er – that one you were telling Dad about the other night," said Amber. "The one that had been badly beaten. Which one is that?"

So she had been listening, thought Erin. She led Amber over to the senior barn and introduced her to Sybil, a little white donkey.

"But she looks fine," said Amber.

"She is now," said Charlie. "But that's only because of Erin's mum's careful nursing." He explained how she'd hand-fed Sybil day and night until the poor little donkey had been strong enough to eat on her own. Her wounds had now healed and she had learned to trust them.

"Her previous owner has been prosecuted for cruelty and banned from keeping animals," Erin told her. "I can show you the pictures of what Sybil looked like when we took her in," she offered.

Amber quickly shook her head. "I don't want to see them."

"Well, there's something you *will* want to see in here," said Erin, and she led her over to the main barn.

In a small stall, was Cherie, with her little foal, Hope.

"Oh, she's so tiny," cried Amber.

Erin told her all about Cherie and how she'd been abandoned.

"I just didn't realize – about all this..." said Amber.

"And we didn't realize about you," said Charlie. "Or we might have tried a bit harder. After all, Benedict didn't give up on you."

"Oh, I know how horrible I am," said Amber. "Everyone gives up on me."

"Except Benedict," said Erin.

"Except Benedict," Amber repeated. "What will happen to him – to all of them – when my father sells the land?"

"We can't find anywhere else where we can care for them," said Erin. "And we can't keep any of them without the fields – donkeys have to have somewhere to graze and to exercise. So Mum and Dad are trying to find new homes for them all."

"And poor Benedict will have to be

moved on," said Charlie.

"But then he'll never trust anyone again." Amber choked back a sob.

"And you won't see Benedict any more," said Erin.

"Unless your father changes his mind," said Charlie.

He looked at Erin and Erin crossed her fingers behind her back.

The spark suddenly came back into Amber's eyes. "He will change his mind – I'll make him."

Erin was a bit afraid to let herself believe what was happening. "D'you really think you can?"

"Oh, I usually get my own way if I kick up enough fuss," she told them.

They walked back towards the main donkey field. Benedict spotted Amber and trotted over to her. They couldn't help laughing as he pushed past Arthur and Clover to get to her.

Once Amber had stroked and patted him he started pawing at the ground with his front foot. Then he suddenly dropped to his knees, turned over on to his back and started rolling on the grass.

"What's the matter with him?" cried Amber. "Is he ill?"

"It's all right," Charlie chuckled. "He's only having a good roll."

"All the donkeys enjoy rolling," said Erin. "But we've never seen Benedict do it before. It must be because he's content now."

"Y-you mean since he's made friends with me?" asked Amber.

Erin nodded. She pointed to a bare patch of earth a little way away. "That's where most of the others roll – they take it in turns. But Benedict has decided to create his own patch."

"Trust Benedict." Amber was smiling at him now.

Hannah was right, thought Erin. *She is pretty when she stops scowling*.

"Right, I'd better go and talk to Dad now," said Amber.

"Great!" said Charlie. "Let us know straight away what he says."

Erin looked up. "Wait a minute – he's here now. That's your father coming out of our house with Mum and Dad."

"What's he doing here?" said Amber.

"Perhaps he's already changed his mind – after the petition and our visit the other night," said Charlie hopefully.

Major Trueman looked up as they all rushed over. "Amber. What—?"

"Have you changed your mind?" Amber interrupted. "You have, haven't you? You're going to let the donkeys stay."

The major looked baffled. "No, I haven't changed my mind."

Erin's mother was wiping her eyes with a tissue. "It's all over," she told Erin. "The land's sold. Major Trueman's just come to tell us we've got four weeks to find new homes for the donkeys."

"Oh, no!" cried Erin.

Chapter 10

Too Late

Amber flew into action. "You can't sell it," she screamed at her father. "The donkeys have got to stay here. Poor Benedict – he'll never trust anyone again. Or Sybil – and then there's Cherie – and Hope."

"What are you talking about?" said Major Trueman. "I thought you hated the donkeys."

"I don't – not now," shouted Amber. "You've got to pull out of this deal – or I'll – I'll –"

"Sulk?" said the major. "Well, it won't work this time. The paperwork is all signed and sealed. It's impossible to pull out at this late stage without the agreement of both parties."

They all listened in shocked silence as he explained that developers had bought the land to build a business park. Apparently several city firms were keen to relocate to the country. "The buildings will only be single-storey and they'll be planting lots of trees and ornamental shrubs to fit in with the surroundings," he told them.

"That's no good to us," said Dad. "The donkeys will still be homeless, and far more countryside will be destroyed than they're planning to replant."

Amber burst into tears. "You've just ruined my life," she cried.

"Don't be such a drama queen," said her father. He was looking quite red and flustered by now. "And anyway it's to keep you happy – you said you wanted to live in a really big house," he told her. "I'm putting the money into a new development. Then next year, when I retire, I'm selling our house and we'll move there. It'll be the sort of house you said you wanted."

Amber stopped crying and stamped her foot hard. "I don't want to move again – I hate moving. I want to stay here."

"But you said you hated it here." Major Trueman shook his head. "Oh, I just don't understand you."

"No, you don't, do you?" shouted Amber. "You've never understood me. Nobody has. The only one who really understands me is – a donkey!" She turned and stamped off.

"But, Amber –" Major Trueman heaved a sigh and turned to Erin's mum and dad. "Look – I'm sorry. I mean, if only – oh, I'd better go after her."

Mum watched him go. "And he had the nerve to call it progress," she said bitterly.

"I can't see what progress there is in making so many people miserable – including his own daughter," said Charlie. "Not to mention twenty-five – no, twenty-seven donkeys."

Dad's eyes were misty. "This is our land. Ours! Mr Benn wanted us to have it for the donkeys. And we can't prove it!"

Erin just stared at them in stunned silence.

Erin and her parents talked well into the night. No one could come up with any solution. Even if by some miracle something turned up they could afford to buy, they still had to find a buyer for their house. The whole process wouldn't be possible in four weeks.

They finally had to come to the heart-breaking decision that they'd have to give up the sanctuary.

Amber arrived before school the next morning to see Benedict. She said that her father was really sorry now and that he would have pulled out of the deal if he could. He'd even phoned the developers last night but they'd insisted on sticking to their agreement.

If only this had all happened just a few days before! thought Erin.

Amber started coming to the sanctuary every day and Benedict was the only one who was happy now. His head was constantly up and his ears pricked. He was in his element and had been doing a lot of rolling in his patch. The grass, which had already been sparse, had worn right away.

"He's making quite a dip in the earth there," said Amber, as she gave him his favourite ginger biscuit.

She was a different girl now. She could still sometimes be a bit prickly but, as

Hannah said, you couldn't expect someone like that to change completely overnight.

The last day of term came, and with it the performance of the nativity play.

Erin looked up at her star. All she could wish for now was that the donkeys would find a new home where they'd be happy and well looked after.

Both Erin's and Charlie's parents came to watch the play but there was no sign of Major Trueman.

The performance actually went very well – in spite of the three miserable-looking angels. Mrs Moffatt had to keep calling "Smile!" from the edge of the stage. Benedict was a big hit and Mrs Moffatt didn't mind when he made people laugh by whipping off Amber's halo. Or even when he insisted on "appearing" to the shepherds in the fields, along with the angels, to deliver "glad tidings of great joy". "It's a happy time, after all," she said to the headmaster. "And who knows? Maybe there really was a donkey in the field then."

The following morning was the first day of the school Christmas holidays and Erin woke up determined to spend as much time with the donkeys as possible. There were now only two weeks before they had to go.

A sanctuary had been found that would take the twenty-two younger donkeys. They'd said it would be a bit of a squeeze but at least the donkeys would be kept together and they'd be well looked after there. Unfortunately, the sanctuary was over two hundred kilometres away, so Erin's family were determined to keep every donkey until the last possible moment.

Charlie and Amber spent all their time at the sanctuary. Ralph and Emma only went home to sleep and Hannah, Matthew and James were regular visitors.

Christmas carols were playing in the village and local people had started bringing Christmas presents of carrots, apples, ginger biscuits and Polo mints for the donkeys. The Christmas lights on the fir trees twinkled at the sanctuary but everyone was existing in a state of numbness. They were all too heartbroken about the donkeys going to even talk about it.

Christmas Eve dawned, still mild for the time of year and there was even a watery sun shining. Only one week to go now, and Erin was hardly sleeping. Every time she closed her eyes she saw the little donkeys' faces. At the front was always Benedict who'd finally learned to trust someone – now that trust was about to be broken.

Charlie arrived early, shortly followed by Amber. Benedict trotted over to see her. Once she'd made a fuss of him he started to paw the ground.

"Look, he's going to start rolling again," said Amber. "He always does that with his hoof first, doesn't he?"

Benedict kept pawing at the soft earth.

Suddenly there was a loud clunk.

"He's hit something hard," said Charlie.

"We must check it out," cried Erin. "He might hurt himself."

Amber climbed over the fence and called to Benedict who obediently went over to her.

Erin called to her father and they went into the field to investigate. Dad scraped the earth away. "It's just a stone," said Erin.

But Dad was still scraping. "A very large stone," he said.

Benedict was looking concerned about what was happening to his rolling patch. "It's all right," said Amber. "There's plenty more field to roll in."

The rest of the donkeys had arrived to watch and were standing round them in a semicircle.

"There's a lot more here," said Dad. "It could be the remains of some old building."

Erin's mind was racing. "I'm going to phone Mrs Moffatt. I bet she'll know what it is."

Chapter 11

An Extremely Important Discovery

Mrs Moffatt came immediately, armed with map, compass, a small trowel and a brush. She seemed really excited as she scraped and brushed, and brushed and scraped. She kept muttering, "It couldn't be... It might be... Could it be? I wonder..."

Eventually there was a piece of stonework at least a metre in length and about thirty centimetres in depth. And it was obvious there was more.

"It has to be!" cried Mrs Moffatt,

suddenly leaping to her feet. She grabbed her mobile phone and started jabbering excitedly into it.

Then she faced the others. "I'm pretty sure this is the lost Roman bathhouse," she told them. "I've just phoned one of my friends from the archaeological society and they're coming over straight away."

Erin smiled at the excited teacher. At least someone was happy.

It seemed only minutes before a Land Rover drew up and two men and a lady jumped out and raced over. They were all just as excited as Mrs Moffatt.

Then there was more scraping and brushing and more measuring and more map-studying. They seemed to be completely unaware of the others watching them – not to mention a row of curious donkeys.

The archaeologists agreed unanimously that these were indeed the ruins of the lost

Roman bathhouse. It was an extremely important discovery!

After that everything started happening. There were lots of phone calls, several journalists arrived and then a television crew.

Mrs Moffatt was interviewed, followed by Erin's parents, then Erin, Charlie and Amber. Benedict was filmed, photographed and treated as a real star, as it had been him that had uncovered the ruins.

It all happened so fast that they were able to watch themselves on the lunchtime news. At least it temporarily took their minds off their troubles.

Mrs Moffatt and the other archaeologists had come into the house to watch the news. They were just finishing cups of tea when Major Trueman burst in.

He was very red in the face and decidedly out of breath. "The developers have been on the phone," he cried. "They've asked if I would agree to cancel the deal."

"They did what? Why? I mean – what did you say?" Dad's words came tumbling out.

"I said yes!" said Major Trueman, beaming at them. "The deal's off. I'm not selling."

Apparently the developers had heard about the discovery of the Roman bathhouse on the news. They said they couldn't afford all the problems and delays that always occur with the discovery of an important archaeological site.

"Whoopee!" cried Erin.

"I can't believe it," said Charlie.

Amber looked as though she was about to burst. Her eyes shone as she faced her father. "So the donkeys are staying?"

The major nodded.

"And us?"

"And us," said her father.

"Brilliant!" cried Erin, tears of joy tumbling down her face.

"Fantastic!" cried Charlie.

Amber rushed to her father and threw her arms round him. He looked a bit surprised – it obviously wasn't something that happened very often.

"That is – just wonderful," said Dad. "But

what about the bathhouse? When that's all been excavated, is there going to be any room for the donkeys?"

"Oh, don't worry about that," said Mrs Moffatt. "You'll only actually lose a small strip of the land you're using. From what we've uncovered this morning, it's clear that the bulk of the bathhouse is under the wooded part of the land."

"It's so lucky that the donkey uncovered it when he did," said another of the archaeologists. "Once the developers got their diggers into that wooded area they could have done untold damage to the stonework."

Everyone was hugging each other.

Then Dad held his hand out to Major Trueman. "I can't thank you enough," he said. "And we'll pay you more rent – like we offered."

The major didn't take his hand. He looked awkward. "Er – this is a bit difficult," he started. "I've got a confession to make."

Oh no, thought Erin. *What now?*

"My uncle – Mr Benn – had mentioned to me that he wanted to leave the land to the donkey sanctuary."

"What?" Amber turned on him. "How could you lie like that?"

"You said you hated it here," he told her. "And well – I didn't think that donkeys were particularly important – at that time."

The rest of them listened in shocked silence as he went on to explain. He'd thought that by selling the land – and eventually the house – he could buy a really expensive property when he retired, the sort he'd thought Amber wanted. He'd hoped that would make her finally settle and be happy.

As his uncle hadn't got around to making a will, he thought he could get away with it.

"Now I can see I was wrong," he admitted. "I'll be signing the land over to you straight after Christmas."

"Oh, wow!" cried Erin. "Thank you."

He looked embarrassed. "I don't deserve your gratitude. I'm just grateful that you've made my daughter happy at last."

"It was Benedict that made her happy," said Charlie.

"It was all of you," said the major. "All of you – and the donkey. You're all such caring people." He walked towards to door. "I can only say I'm very, very sorry. I'll keep out of your way in future."

"No!" Dad grabbed him by the arm. "You don't have to keep out of our way. What you did was wrong. But it was because you cared for your daughter."

"You've made it right now," said Mum. "And we'd like you and Amber to join us tomorrow – for Christmas dinner."

"Whoopee!" cried Amber. "I can't remember ever having a proper family Christmas." She thanked Erin's mum for the invitation and then ran outside and headed for the field, closely followed by Erin and Charlie.

"Guess what?" she told Benedict. "You're staying. I'm staying."

"You're all staying!" Charlie called across the field to the other donkeys.

"And it's all thanks to you, Benedict." Erin threw her arms round the little donkey's shaggy neck.

"You'll have more money now you won't have to pay any rent," said Charlie. "Plus we'll be able to get the adoption scheme going."

"And maybe more donations – from visitors coming to see the Roman bathhouse," said Amber.

"We'll be able to help even more donkeys," said Erin.

"This is going to be such a great Christmas!" Amber told Benedict.

They stood silently watching the other

donkeys. John, Paul, George and Ringo were having another pow-wow, Joseph was rolling, Clover was following Arthur across the field, and Tapestry was resting her head on Fred's back. In the far field the elderly donkeys were chewing contentedly on some hay.

Suddenly Lucy-May and Chocolate cantered across the field in front of them, kicking up their back hoofs. Benedict called after them. "Hee-haw. Hee-haw."

They all laughed.

Mrs Moffatt came up and gathered all three children in a big hug. "How lovely to see my three Christmas angels so happy."

"I still can't believe it," said Erin. "Less than twenty-four hours ago everything was so bad but now," she turned to Charlie, "we've really got our Christmas wish, haven't we?"

"You know what I think?" said Mrs Moffatt. "I think there must have been real angels around this Christmas Eve."

Look out for this special Christmas book
by Sylvia Green:

Sylvia Green

The Best
Christmas
Ever

Two Christmas stories in one book for £4.99!

SCHOLASTIC